by Johanna Spyri

Eveli

By Johanna Spyri

Translated by Helen B. Dole

Cover illustration by Katherine Blackmore

Cover Design by Elle Staples

© 2019 Jenny Phillips
Originally published in 1926
This unabrideged version has been updated with mordern spelling and punctuation.
www.thegoodandthebeautiful.com

Table of Contents

Chapter 1: At the Nettle-Farmer's 1

Chapter 2: Eveli Makes an Acquaintance 10

Chapter 3: A New Sorrow 23

Chapter 4: In the Hospital 33

Chapter 5: The Nettle-Farmer's Surprise 47

Chapter 1: At the Nettle-Farmer's

"In the Forest" was the name of the last house, standing somewhat higher than all the others, surrounded by meadows and fields lying scattered here and there on the mountains, the slope of which was covered with the woods called the forest. If the grass up here was not so rich as below in the valley abounding in fruit and corn, it was so sweet that when it lay cut on the meadows, the whole air all around was filled with its fragrance.

The house in the forest was not one of the large farmhouses, but one of the most beautiful meadows extended from it far down the mountainside, and the big potato field behind the house yielded from the dry ground a rich harvest of very excellent tubers.

Why the owner was called the nettle-farmer no one could exactly say; some thought there were a great many nettles on his land, but others said it was because his words usually hurt like stinging nettles. He himself was not displeased to be so called, for he knew only about the first explanation, and it seemed to him right that the people should believe his land bore nettles and not the fair grass and abundant potatoes which he harvested.

In his barn, built next to the house, stood two cows beside the indispensable goat, but there would be room for three. The farmer often thought of himself and reckoned that with one good summer more, an abundant crop of hay and the milk which he could furnish to the cowherd's hut, enough would be realized for him to purchase a third cow. His brother-in-law below on the mountain had three; why should he not get ahead as far as him? He had in mind still another plan which he was agitating. The nettle-farmer had many plans; he was always planning. He had two boys, twelve and fourteen years old, both of whom were already working industriously with him, and now the younger one was ready to leave school and could work with him all day.

If his livestock should be increased somewhat, he could make good use of the piece of land adjoining his sunny meadow, and even more valuable than this, he could acquire the land, he knew. The owner would sell it; he already had enough work, alone as he was, without wife or child. But then he could make good use of a third boy for the increased work, the nettle-farmer reckoned still further, for he would never employ strangers. But he did not know why he should not have three boys, he said to himself. His brother-in-law had three and two daughters besides, but daughters he did not long for. The work which fell to his wife she accomplished alone, promptly and quietly as well; such young ladies would waste their time in gossiping and be always wanting something; this he knew for certain. But a boy he could make use of. This was the clear result of his reckoning.

Sure enough, not long after this, when he came home from work, his wife called to him:

"Come in and see the pretty baby that has come." And as he stepped in she said:

"But it is not a boy, it is a little daughter."

This vexed the farmer very much, for he had not counted on it.

"Do what you like with it," he said and went out again.

When Sunday drew near, and the child was to be taken to the village and baptized, the mother asked:

"What shall the child be called? We haven't decided anything about it."

Then the father replied:

"You can call her Eva, for she has above all brought one person misfortune."

The wife seldom answered back, but this time she said:

"The little one really did not come specially to bring you misfortune, but she can be called Eva all the same; I like the name."

So the little one was baptized Eva and afterwards called Eveli. Eveli grew and was a very docile and unusually tender-hearted child. She avoided every little creature in her way or quickly jumped over it in order not to step on it. If she came across one that was wounded or half dead, she had no peace until she had placed it gently on a soft leaf so that it looked very comfortable in its pretty bed. So Eveli had many little friends around the house, for it seemed as if all the creatures wanted to return the kindness shown to them. They hopped and flew around Eveli everywhere, and when she held out grain or crumbs in her open palm the birds would come flying along and peck them quite trustfully out of her hand. But when people came, Eveli quickly fled into the house, and even indoors she would look around shyly, as soon as she heard a footstep. But this was not to be wondered at, for wherever there were people, Eveli always felt that she was in the wrong place. From the time when she was little, if she was running around and her father came along, he would say sharply:

"Don't be always in the way, you little good-for-nothing thing, you!"

And later on the two brothers, Heini and Lieni, also began to do likewise and even much oftener than their father, for it was so convenient when one was vexed about one's work—or they were angry with each other—to give vent to their feelings in this way. So they always cried out even before they really came near Eveli, first one and then the other:

"Don't always be getting in the way, you good-for-nothing thing, you!"

So Eveli came to feel that wherever she was with people, she was in the way. This made Eveli very shy and afraid of everybody, except her mother. She was never unfriendly and never gave her a cross word. But she heard very few other words from her, for she had to work hard all day long, and in the evening she was so tired that she fell asleep immediately when she lay down beside Eveli.

When Eveli had passed her sixth year and spring was approaching, the farmer's wife said one day to her husband, "We must think what to do; the child must go to school after Easter."

"There is nothing to think about. She will go to school then, and that is all there is about it," retorted her husband.

"She is still too little and not strong enough to make the trip four times a day," said his wife further. "She must stay down at noon. We must ask someone about it."

"Not to send her to school would be the most sensible way," growled her husband.

"I think so, too; but what if the notice comes up from below telling what we have to do?" replied his wife calmly.

"Then send her to your brother."

Whereupon her husband went away. His wife knew very well that her brother down in the village was the only one whom they could ask, and also the nearest; but her husband himself had to make the decision or else he would never think she had done right—this she knew very well. So on Sunday afternoon she took Eveli by the hand, for she had to learn the right way down the mountain to her relatives in Unterwies. No one was at home except the old grandmother, the mother of the nettle-farmer's wife, who lived with her son. She was very much delighted to see her daughter again, for she left her house so rarely that her mother hardly saw her twice in the year, since she could no longer go up to the forest. She was delighted also that she would now learn to know her granddaughter, Eveli, and it pleased her very much that from Easter on she would come every day to her.

Her son's five children were already grown—Hans, the youngest, was sixteen years old. Eveli was unspeakably relieved when she heard that all five, and the father and mother besides, were away. She had trembled all over at that thought of the moment when she would have to go in before all these people, and have to greet them. But the grandmother was so kind and so old, and she trembled, too, all the time, as Eveli could easily see; perhaps she was frightened, also. Eveli at once felt great confidence in her.

The grandmother thought her daughter would do well to wait for her brother and his wife to make arrangements with them herself; but the woman was in a hurry to get home again; her husband was not accustomed to having her go away, and he had surely been expecting her back for a long time, she said.

The grandmother could tell them about the matter, she thought, and if no objection was made, from Easter on Eveli would come to them every day at noon-time. The grandmother promised to speak in behalf of the arrangement. She was delighted to have Eveli come. The child in her quiet way would surely be frightened to be in an entirely strange place, but with her she would feel at home, she thought. Eveli would like to come down to the grandmother, if only she was alone, but in her heart she had great fear of the cousins and her aunt, the old and the young, and kept hoping that it would be a long time before Easter. But Easter came along very quickly, and Eveli had to begin going to school. When she appeared for the first time at dinner with her cousins and had to sit down at the table with so many people, she was so timid that she did not dare lift her eyes and could hardly swallow her food from sheer fright before all the faces looking at her. If she was asked a question, she gave such a low answer that she could hardly be understood, and when they rose from the table, she had no idea where to stand, for she was so afraid they would all say immediately that she was in the way. After a few days, the young cousins began to tease her at the table.

One would say: "Have you never learned to talk, Eveli, or don't you need to up there; do they do something else?" And another would say:

"Perhaps they do up there like the birds in the forest; they chirp instead of talk."

Then they would all laugh very hard, and their sisters would laugh loud, too; and one would say Eveli must begin singing;

she must be a canary bird. They had wanted one for a long time. This would make them all laugh so loud that Eveli was completely paralyzed with fright.

"Stop teasing now," said the grandmother; "if you don't mean any harm, you can surely see how frightened she is."

But every day there would be a little teasing, for Eveli did not learn to talk, and sat so doubled up at the table that the young cousin Hans said she looked exactly like a closed pocketknife, which called forth a loud peal of laughter.

After dinner, one after another soon went out, to work in the kitchen, in the field, or the garden; only the grandmother was left behind. Then she seated herself at her spinning wheel, and there always came a beautiful hour for Eveli until she had to go back to school. She sat down in the safe corner behind the grandmother's spinning wheel, and the grandmother would tell her something about the time when she herself was a child, as Eveli was now, or talked kindly with her, or often said, "Now let us sing together a little while."

Eveli liked this especially, for although the grandmother's voice was a little shaky, the songs sounded just as beautifully in Eveli's ears, and she liked to sing with her, for she enjoyed singing above everything else. She herself had a pure, clear voice, and although it was not very strong, it was as musical as a little bell. The grandmother liked to listen when the soft voice sang her old songs, which she no longer heard any more. Eveli always warmed up and was able to tell about all sorts of things when she was alone so with the grandmother, while she never dared speak a word before her cousins and aunt, and became more and more shy with them the more they tried to make her talk by teasing. When she flew away like a timid bird as quickly as possible from the table into the corner where the spinning wheel stood and the grandmother would immediately sit down again, then she often said to her:

"You see, Eveli, they don't do it to hurt you; they only want to make each other laugh, and you should laugh with them." But that was not possible to Eveli.

Chapter 2: Eveli Makes an Acquaintance

After school, when Eveli went up the mountain, there was always ahead of her a crowd of boys who, with a great noise and much jumping to one side, were going back the same way. They were boys from the different farms lying scattered on the mountain. Here and there one of the crowd would disappear. His goal was reached or he had to continue his way by a side path. Towards the top of the mountain the crowd always became smaller, and finally Eveli climbed in silence and alone to the forest. The crowd always remained large halfway up the mountain, and Eveli held back and crept along close to the hedge so that she would not be seen by the boys. There, at the end of the hedge, just before a troop of them turned aside, something remarkable happened every day. Eveli could not really grasp what it was; there the procession stopped every time, a loud singing and strange noise began and lasted a little while, then a tremendous laughter broke forth, and then, still laughing boisterously, the boys ran away in different directions. Eveli wondered a little what always happened there, although she was terribly afraid of the noisy boys. Today, she had come somewhat nearer to them than usual; they had so many side-springs to make. Then came the little house somewhat aside from the path. A large birch tree stood beside it. There the noise broke forth every time. The boys were all armed with long hazel-rods; this Eveli could see very well. She went quickly forward a little way, then stooped down behind the crooked apple tree by the path.

Then it burst forth; with frightfully raised voices the boys all sang together in strict time:

There sits humpback Beni,

There sits humpback Ben;

Three times three is nine

And one is ten.

Those behind beat time on the schoolbags of those in front of them so hard that it resounded and cracked, and the rods flew in pieces. Then the singers had to laugh so uproariously that they didn't move from the spot for quite a while. Then suddenly they all began to scatter up and away.

Then Eveli came out from behind the tree; she looked searchingly over to the house to see if anyone was in sight there. She saw nothing; the door was standing open, but no one was there. But nearby, under the big birch tree, stood a little chair close up to the trunk. Something small was sitting in it that moved. Eveli ventured a little nearer; now everything could be plainly seen. In the chair sat a little humpbacked boy with black hair, and he was looking over with inquiring eyes at Eveli. To him the boys had sung their song; this was quite clear now to Eveli. She had a beautiful red flower in her hand. The grandmother had broken the flower from her plant in the window and given it to Eveli because she had always looked so longingly at the beautiful blossoms.

Then Eveli suddenly ran to the birch tree, quickly laid the flower on the little boy's knee, and ran away without looking round, as if she had done something which ought to frighten her.

On the following afternoon, when she was again passing the same way, she heard nothing of the noise and laughter of the day before. Perhaps the boys had gone so far ahead of her that she could not hear them, or perhaps the child was not sitting there, so they had not sung.

Eveli wondered very much whether he was there. She had to go a little nearer, as she had done the day before.

Suddenly, from the birch tree sounded a call: "Come over here to me!"

Eveli timidly drew back a few steps. She would have run away, but the call sounded again and so entreatingly: "Do come over here to me!"

Then Eveli went slowly towards the birch tree, looking cautiously around her to see if anyone else was there. In the little chair sat a pale and very deformed boy. Near to, he looked older than Eveli had supposed, as from a distance she thought he was a very little boy.

"Come nearer to me," he said when Eveli again stood still from shyness. She obeyed. The boy looked at her very earnestly with his searching, gray eyes. The pale little face was so thin and bore such an expression of suffering that it went deep to Eveli's heart.

"Why did you bring me the flower?" he now asked.

"Because they sang so to you and then laughed," answered Eveli.

"Yes, and I am not to blame," said the boy.

"For what?" asked Eveli.

"For the humpback. They laugh at me for that."

The little boy looked up at Eveli with his earnest eyes so searchingly, as if he wanted to ask whether she, too, felt like laughing.

"Yes, I know how it is," she said sympathetically.

"No, you don't know that; you haven't a humpback." The boy had at once looked at the child's back.

"But I have other things that make them laugh, and they do laugh at me, too, you can believe," said Eveli.

"What for?" asked the boy.

"Because I can't talk before so many people, and because I am always in everybody's way," answered Eveli.

"You must just get out of their way," exclaimed the boy.

"I can't; only the others can do that, but I really cannot," asserted Eveli, "when I want to so much. But you know perhaps they don't mean to do any harm," she quickly added, as if to console herself and him; "they only want to do something to make them all have a great laugh together."

"Do you think so?" said the boy. "What is your name?"

"Eveli, and what is yours?"

"Beni. Didn't you hear what they sang?"

"Yes, to be sure; but I did not know if it was true what they sang, or only made up. Are you always alone?"

"Yes. Father only comes home to sleep, and early in the morning he goes away again to work."

"Where is your mother, then?"

"I haven't any, only an aunt; but she never hears anything; she is always inside in the house. Will you come again tomorrow to see me?"

"Yes, if you are so alone, I really will," said Eveli, who was on the point of hurrying away.

"Will you come every afternoon?" asked Beni imploringly.

"Yes, if you would like to have me, I will come," said Eveli hastily, for now she had to run; she had lingered some time in talking. Eveli felt a joy in her heart such as she had never known before. There was somebody in the world that was glad to have her come to him again, and it was a poor, sick boy of whom she did not need at all to be afraid. As soon as she reached home, she ran to her mother to tell her everything and to ask if she might go to Beni every afternoon and stay a little while with him. For a long time her mother could not listen, as she had to hurry from the washing to strain the milk, from there to the little pigs, and from these to peel potatoes in the kitchen. Here Eveli finally reached her and told her experience and made her request. Her mother was glad to allow Eveli this pleasure; nobody at home asked after the child, and if she came home early or late, nobody cared except her.

Eveli could hardly wait the next day until the noisy boys had finished their uproar and had scattered so that she could venture to go ahead. Beni held out his thin hand to her.

"Today I didn't care when they sang, because I knew that you would come along behind them and would hear them, and because you think they only do so in order to make each other laugh hard," he said. "Will you stay with me a little while now?"

Eveli was glad to do so and sat down on the ground beside the chair. Beni wanted so much to know what happened in school and how it was when one could read, and if Eveli believed she would soon be able to read a story out of a book and understand what someone had told him. His aunt had told him once that was what they learned in school, and when he got well and had strength in his legs to walk, he too could go to school and learn everything like other children.

"But I never can do that," added Beni sadly. "I don't gain any strength; I can't stand up."

Then Eveli understood why he always had two little crutches standing beside him. Poor Beni was not only humpbacked, he could not stand or walk; he could only hop around leaning on his crutches. This seemed frightful to Eveli; with anguish in her heart, she tried to think of some consolation.

"When you are bigger you will surely be stronger," she said, persuading herself conclusively. "Then you can always go to school; you are surely not so very old."

"I am already nine years old," said Beni quite earnestly, shaking his head.

"Well, that is nothing," continued Eveli hastily. "You know what we can do until you are able to come to school, too? I will come to you every day, and then I will show you each time what we have learned, what letters and what strokes to write.

You know I can't read very well yet, but the teacher often tells us a story. I will tell you about it; then it will be exactly as if you could come to school."

Beni's eyes, usually so anxious and sad, shone with delight.

"Do you think that I really can learn to read and then read all the stories in the books and understand them?" he asked, quite excited over such a promising prospect.

"Yes, to be sure, just as we do in school. I will really pay strict attention so that I shall not forget anything," promised Eveli. "I won't forget a thing, so you can follow everything right. Shall we begin right away?"

Beni trembled with longing for his first instruction, and never before had a child undertaken his first pencil mark with such rapture as Beni today executed his.

Something entirely new had come into Beni's life. When he woke in the morning, he saw something before him which he could delight in; this he had never known before. All day long he looked with hope in his heart towards evening. Every day now he listened with the greatest longing for the boys' noisy song; it was the sure sign that Eveli was coming immediately. As soon as the boys had roughly scattered, she always stepped from behind the apple tree and came running along. Then work began at once, and Beni went at it with such eagerness that Eveli could never give him enough to learn. He always kept asking,

"Haven't you learned something more?"

If Eveli then began to think it over, she often found something more that she had forgotten. Then Beni's eyes would light up in joy as if a new stroke to a letter was a matchless jewel.

"Perhaps we shall soon come to the reading, Eveli. Think how that will be!" he said, beaming with happiness. "Just think, then we can read what is in every book. Do you think there are many books? Is there always something more to read as long as you live?"

"Yes, indeed, naturally," answered Eveli with assurance. "Only think, in school each class has its own books, no two alike, and the children who can read go every Sunday to the pastor and bring home a book to read; just think, each one has one, and every Sunday each one goes again and brings home a new book and never, never the same."

Beni was very much amazed that there were so many books, and his desire increased more and more to get ahead where he would be able to read what was in these books. This desire was increased by the beautiful stories, which Eveli repeated after the teacher every few days. They were so exciting and filled all his thoughts, but they always came to an end so soon that Beni felt a real pain every time Eveli said: "Now that is the end."

But these delighted Beni the whole week long. There was

something else Beni learned through Eveli, a pleasure which brought the tears to his eyes every time, yet delighted his heart. Beni had never heard singing, for the boys' daily screaming "There sits humpback Beni" could hardly be called so. Eveli had often told him about her stay with her cousins at noon-time and how glad she was every day when all the others left the room and she had quite a while all alone with her grandmother, who was always so kind and sang songs with her.

Then Beni was very eager to know how this singing sounded, and when Eveli sang to him in her soft, musical voice for the first time, bright tears ran down Beni's cheeks, from the beginning to the end. After that he felt there was nothing more beautiful, and every day when Eveli insisted there was nothing more to learn, he begged urgently:

"But please sing me a song, or just one verse, or please sing two!"

And he would look up at Eveli so longingly that she could never deny the request, although she thought sometimes it was too late after all the spelling. When Eveli sang again, Beni would sit as if absorbed, and he was unaware that his eyes had filled with tears.

When Eveli asked him what she should sing, he would say every time:

"The song about spring."

Eveli was always willing to do what he wished, and she sang immediately what she had already sung to him a hundred times before:

All the birds once more are trilling,

Welcome spring, welcome spring!

Their sweet notes, my chamber filling,

Bid me sing, bid me sing!

What can such a call betoken,

Songster free, songster free!

See! My wings are torn and broken,

Woe is me! Woe is me!

Still may song the sick heart lighten.

In thy room, in thy room.

Wings may fail, but prayer will brighten

Darkest gloom, darkest gloom.

Thou canst feel the sunbeams glancing,

Warm and sweet, warm and sweet.

See them on the tree-tops dancing

With gay feet, with gay feet!

What was cold and dry has taken

New life on, new life on;

Blossoms everywhere awaken,

Winter's gone, winter's gone!

For thee also spring is given,

Trust to love, trust to love!

Thou shalt soar to azure heaven,

Far above, far above!

After this, if there was still time and Eveli did not have to run away at once in order to be home for supper, when her father and brothers would return, Beni usually asked:

"Now sing about getting well!" And if Eveli thought she could, she would sing also:

Keep a brave heart,

Even with many a sorrow

Griefs soon depart.

Near a kind Savior thou art,

Wait—He will help thee tomorrow.

Do not lament

Even though clouds lower thickly,

Storms are soon spent.

When night is gone, follow quickly

Radiant day and content.

Sorrow and pain

Are not for lasting intended.

After the rain

Bright comes the sunshine again—

Soon will thy illness be mended!

Chapter 3: A New Sorrow

About this time everybody near the nettle-farmer was having a hard life. Even the two boys, whom he usually praised for their work, could no longer do anything right for him. The two were so cross about it that they had to vent their ill-humor on somebody. There was no one there except Eveli, who now could go and stay where she liked, so she had not to hear from her father or brothers that she was everywhere in the way, and besides was now much too big; she could do something better.

The nettle-farmer had attained his desire; he had been able to buy a third cow, and with his two grown sons had accomplished all the work to be done so well that he could now purchase the fine piece of land that he had had his eye on for a long time. He knew that his neighbor intended to sell it as soon as a buyer came along who could pay for it at once; and he could do it, for he had thought and reckoned about it day and night for seven years, and he and all belonging to him had pinched as much as possible to lay aside every penny for the purchase of the piece of land, which would bring in so much that later on they would be better off than ever before. Therefore, they could well spare a little now, he said.

So one Sunday he went over to the neighbor's to bargain with him. The man lived all alone; he had never married and for years had looked after everything alone, his barn, his fields, and his house. However, his work had become somewhat too much for him with the years, or he would not have thought of parting with his beautiful piece of land, he had said himself. Until now no purchaser had actually appeared. When the nettle-farmer entered his house and made his proposal, the neighbor's eyes shot fiery glances from his disheveled hair and shaggy beard at him, and he said he was surprised that the nettle-farmer should have the impudence to ask him to sell his land. He would have nothing to do with him, and the nettle-farmer should know why. Then he showed him the door and said nothing more.

The nettle-farmer went out; he saw there was nothing to be done. He had made a mistake when he supposed that his neighbor would long ago have gotten over what had happened twenty years before. A pear tree stood on the boundary between their two fields, which adjoined, and both farmers claimed it as his. Since they could not agree about it, they went to law; the tree was awarded to the nettle-farmer. Since the nettle-farmer had won, the matter had long ago been dismissed from his mind, and he assumed his neighbor would have done the same. But his neighbor had lost and had never gotten over the loss of his pear tree, and every time he looked at it his anger towards the nettle-farmer rose anew.

Since this Sunday when the neighbor had turned him away, no one could any longer please the nettle-farmer, and it seemed as if he became more and more morose. He could think of nothing else day and night except how he could arrange to get possession of the piece of land for which he had toiled and saved and struggled for seven years, as if for the highest good, the possession of which would sweeten all endeavors. Now that he saw himself at his goal, it could not be possible that everything had been to no purpose, all at an end, everything in vain; it was not to be borne. The one he coveted was a fine piece of land, really the most productive on the whole mountain. It not only lay in the full sun at midday but it stretched away on the mountain towards the west and had the last rays of the setting sun. Brooding gloomily, the nettle-farmer went around revolving his single desire again and again until he came to the decision to offer his neighbor what he would not refuse. The piece of land he must have, even if he had to work three full years more for it and would not possess a penny of ready money afterwards. This land, with its fertile soil, this single beautiful piece of land must be his possession.

One Sunday evening, when twilight was coming on, the nettle-farmer went a second time to his neighbor's house; in bright daylight he did not care to go. The house stood rather far away on the western slope of the mountain and a good piece farther down. His neighbor was called the middle-farmer, because his farm was not up in the forest, neither did it lie down on the mountain. He was standing in the barn door when the nettle-farmer came along. The nettle-farmer walked slowly to the barn:

"I have come once more about buying the land," he said. "I

think we could agree about it."

"You know my mind," said the other without moving.

"I can pay even more than you stipulated for the land."

"It makes no difference."

"I will pay a quarter more and half in cash."

"What I have said, you know."

"How much do you want for it? I will give even more; say what the last price is."

Then the middle-farmer burst forth:

"You cannot have my land, even if I should have to become a beggar! And if you stand here until New Year's and keep on asking, you will get no other answer; now you know." Whereupon the middle-farmer turned his back to his neighbor and went over to his house.

The nettle-farmer was so angry that he doubled up both fists, but there was nothing to be done. This was the end of the plan he had cherished so many years. He went home as if he had been dealt his death blow.

Although this was a very bad time, and Eveli did not know where to put her feet without making somebody angry, yet in her heart she had one consolation—she could spend every afternoon with her friend, and see what delight Beni always, always found in her coming! Meanwhile mid-summer had come. Today the teacher had told the children in school that the next week vacation would begin, and they would not have to come any more for six weeks. This was great news, which Eveli had to bring to Beni. Now the bright daylight lasted so long, perhaps she would be allowed to come to him early in the afternoon. So how many lovely hours they would have to spend together! Eveli hurried up the mountain after school and, as soon as the way was clear, to the birch tree. Beni sat weeping pitifully in his chair. He could hardly bring out his "Good evening, Eveli," in the midst of his sobs.

"What is the matter, Beni; what is the matter? Has anyone hurt you?" asked Eveli, quite shocked.

"Oh, it is all over," he sobbed. "You can never come any more; we can never be together any more. I have to go away. It is all over, all over."

Eveli was surprised and shocked to the highest degree.

"Where must you go? Why must you go away? Who has told you so?" she asked in succession with the greatest excitement.

But she had to wait a while until Beni, to whom now in Eveli's presence the matter appeared for the first time in all its sadness, could collect himself sufficiently to be able to give a connected story of what had happened. He sometimes had attacks when he became unconscious and fell off his chair. If the aunt happened to come out, for she could not hear him at all, she would lift him up and place him in his chair again, or bring him in to his bed, where he would come to himself again.

Today he had fallen down very early in the morning, Beni went on to say, and when he came to he was still lying on the ground and could not get up, and he could not bring out his aunt no matter how loud he cried. And it hurt him so badly in his side, and still hurt him. A long time afterwards his aunt came out and at first he could hardly sit up, and had shown her where it hurt him so, and then she had said she must go to the doctor, and had gone. Then she brought back word that they must take him down to the hospital right away, tomorrow morning. There he would have to stay a long time; the doctor had ordered it.

This was sad news for Eveli, too. Just now in the beautiful vacation time everything would be broken up; she would not be able to go to Beni anymore, for a very long while, perhaps no more all summer. Eveli could find no consolation. She sat on the ground beside Beni's chair and then she saw how sad he looked, and she thought how tomorrow he would have to go down to the big hospital among entire strangers, and perhaps would never come back; then Eveli also began to cry softly, and Beni, who had not entirely stopped, began to sob pitifully again. Today they could not study any more, neither could they sing a note.

The next morning, when Eveli, on her way to school, looked over, the little chair was no longer under the birch tree, so it was really true; Beni had already been taken away early in the morning to the hospital. Then Eveli felt such a choking in her throat as if she must scream aloud. But to go to school with weeping eyes, no, that she must not do. She ran with all her might down the mountain.

In the afternoon Eveli was able to pour out her troubles to the grandmother, after her young cousin Hans had teased her at the table by saying: "Eveli must be a little nun. Every day she drops her eyes lower to the ground, and at last she will not open them at all; then she will have to bore her way along, like a mole," whereupon an uproarious laughter followed.

She told the grandmother everything, what had happened to Beni, and how he had now disappeared, perhaps forever, so that she would never see him again. But the grandmother said Eveli must not forget what she had already told her, that when the dear Lord sends people something hard to bear, He always lays a blessing underneath, which one may not see right away, because the burden hides it, but when that is taken away it comes forth, and one can at last be thankful for everything. Now Eveli must think only about Beni and not of herself and that going to the hospital will be a great benefit to the poor boy. There he will have good care and not be so neglected as at home, where his father is away from early till late, and he could never talk with the deaf aunt, and never call her when he needed help so badly. Eveli really would have done so and only thought of Beni, if he had not been so inconsolable himself because he had to go.

On her way home she hurried breathlessly past the place where she could see the birch tree. She could not bear to look over where everything was so empty. She had four days more to go over the path, then Sunday would come and vacation begin. Thinking of the many lovely afternoons which she could have spent in the coming vacation with Beni, she had to shed many tears during the four days of going to school.

On Sunday morning Eveli crouched down as low as she could in the window corner with her red cornflowers, the lovely petals of which she wanted to lay in her mother's singing book and dry. Eveli knew very well why she crouched down so low and hid. It was the time when her brothers would come in to their affairs of Sunday neckties, collar buttons, and what their mother might produce of Sunday finery. They were both usually in a hurry to be ready before their father came because he would say they didn't need to want such foolishness. So Eveli knew very well that she must hide, so as not to be in the way. Then the door was opened with considerable noise and a firm step came in. Eveli looked under the table through to the door, to see which one it was; it was neither of her brothers, but her young cousin Hans.

"Good morning, Aunt! Where is Eveli?" he asked as he came in. "She must have put her head under her wing and hid in the straw when she saw me coming. But it's of no use; she must come out!" Then he had to laugh hard because Eveli really came out of the corner as frightened as if she came out of hiding in the straw.

"So you ventured to come out?" he continued, still laughing. "Grandmother sent me. She said if it wasn't for you and me, nobody would give her any pleasure anymore. We are two brave ones, aren't we? She sent word for you to come down to the hospital, if Aunt has no objection."

Eveli did not know what she heard; was it really true? Would she be allowed to visit Beni in the hospital? She looked inquiringly at her mother. She nodded kindly and said:

"Yes, yes, surely you may go."

"When?" asked Eveli, still uncertain about the good fortune.

"Today at two o'clock, and again later; that much I understood," stated Hans.

"Is it to see Beni? May I go there to Beni?" asked Eveli, not quite sure of the matter.

"To Benjamin Lorch, Unterwies Hospital," said Hans solemnly.

Eveli was so delighted she did not know what she ought to say to Hans.

"Would you like an early pear?" came out like a sudden inspiration.

"Yes, indeed," laughed Hans, "but you really haven't any; they are not yet at all ripe."

But her mother had early that day discovered the first ripe

fruit on the topmost branch of the pear tree which turned so beautifully to the sun. She had knocked it down and brought it to Eveli. She now took the pear out of her pocket and held it out to Hans. It was red and yellow and round as a ball it was so ripe.

"Gracious, see the beauty!" exclaimed Hans, seized it, and with his firm teeth bit so hard into the soft pear that it squirted and cracked, again and again until with skin and core it disappeared.

"That was the best pear I ever ate in my whole life," said Hans with satisfaction, "so full of juice and so warm. Now I will always take your part, Eveli, when you are with us, and if the others laugh at you again I will laugh at them so hard and say such things to their faces that they will have to be glad when I keep still again. You will see, Eveli, how that will work! From now on I will keep with you, count on it! Now I must go home, goodbye!"

Whereupon he left the house, and Eveli looked after him, filled with gratitude. She had suddenly won a protector in him; she did not know how, but she was so glad about it.

Chapter 4: In the Hospital

Eveli thought today it would never be twelve o'clock, when the short dinner would be ready, and after that she could go. But twelve o'clock came even today, and as soon as her father and brothers had finished their meal and had left the room again, she ran to her mother in the kitchen and asked quickly:

"May I go now?"

Her mother thought there was no hurry; it would be almost two hours before two o'clock, and she would not be allowed to go into the hospital earlier. But still she allowed her to go, for she saw that the child would have no more peace, and she must wait down below; she could go to her grandmother until it was time. Then Eveli ran off. Eveli had never before seen everything as beautiful outdoors as it was today. The bright red morning glories were climbing everywhere in the shining hawthorn hedge; the thyme wafted its fragrance from under all the hedges and on the green mountain slope which shimmered in the sun. But where the fields began, there was the most beautiful sight of all. There the blue cornflowers looked out from among the tall corn with such merry eyes, and the red poppies gleamed and shone next to them and behind and on every side. Eveli must have some flowers, the red ones and the blue; there were so many they would surely delight Beni now that he could not sit outdoors anymore and could not see the flowers and meadows and hedges any longer. Eveli was so eager to take Beni as many as she could reach of the beautiful flowers that she picked and picked, and yet there were more even lovelier ones still coming in sight; whole plants of beautiful flowers were to be seen farther on, and there they blazed like fire from the red through the green corn. Eveli must have these, and still more of the blue; over there were the most beautiful of all. But now her bouquet was so big that she could hardly clasp it any longer with both hands. She went on farther; she could not run anymore; the flowers would not allow it; but it was quite right; she would not have to wait so long before the door of the hospital. Eveli had spent more time picking flowers than she realized. Just as she was coming into the village and was going back of the churchyard across the meadow to the hospital, it struck two from the church tower. So Eveli could go at once into the isolated house, around which it was very still. One of the nurses came out.

"Are you Eveli, who would like to visit Beni?" she asked kindly. "If so, come right in with me."

She opened the door. Eveli stepped into a room where there were a number of white beds; in some sick children were lying; others were empty. She looked all around; there in a lovely, clean bed, Beni was sitting up and smiled with sparkling eyes over at Eveli. She ran to him and laid her big bouquet of flowers in front of him. Eveli had seen that a door was standing open into another room, but she had not looked in there, and hurried straight to Beni's bed. But the red and blue flowers had shone in as she passed by, and a beseeching voice now called out:

"Bring me just one of them, only one!"

Eveli understood what was meant and looked questioningly at Beni. She had brought them all as a present for him. Then he took out two blue and two red ones from the bunch and said:

"Take all the rest to them. They must be suffering so much in there; I hear them really groaning."

The sister, who was standing near, came along and said it would be all right if Eveli wished to do so, and she would go with her. Then Eveli seized her huge bouquet again and followed the sister into the other room. It was a large ward, with many more beds in it than in Beni's room, and in almost every bed lay a sick woman. When Eveli came in with her shining bouquet they cried from all sides: "Oh, how lovely! Oh, how lovely! Oh, bring me just one! And me one!" Then Eveli went from one bed to another and always laid two flowers on every cover, one red and one blue, and the pale women looked at Eveli so thankfully and all held their flowers in their hands so it looked as if there was a great festival in the hospital. But even after the distribution, Eveli still had a large bunch in her hand; she had gathered such a quantity of flowers. She looked questioningly at the sister, to see if she should begin giving them out again. The sister took Eveli by the hand.

"Come, you can give still more pleasure," she said and went with her to the door.

Then the women called to her: "Come to us again! Please, will you come again?" And Eveli was glad to promise that she would come again. Such happiness as now filled Eveli's heart she had never before experienced. All the suffering women wished she would come again, and she could bring them something every day to make them happy. The sister went with Eveli through the corridor and opened another door. Again she stepped into a large ward which was full of beds; in there lay young men with wasted faces and also quite old men with gray beards and snow-white hair.

Eveli stood still for a moment in the doorway, but one of them immediately called: "Come along, you must not be afraid. Will you give me one of the flowers, too?"

Then, so many voices called even more longingly than the women. One exclaimed:

"Oh, the cornflowers! Oh, could I see the cornflowers? Give me just one of the blue ones!"

And so many of them called and begged and thanked Eveli so heartily when she laid two flowers on their bed, just as the women had done!

In the farthest corner lay one more that frightened Eveli a little; his hair and his beard looked so wild. He sat up in his bed and looked with such sharp eyes at the flowers that Eveli grew more and more frightened and felt perhaps she was in the way. She stood still and considered whether she ought to turn away.

"Come here, come here; I won't hurt you," said the sick man as he held out his hand longingly to the child. "Show them to me, if you don't care to give them to me, but put one in my hand. There, thank you, you are a good little child. Where did you get them? On the mountain, did you say? The fine corn will soon be ripe, and I cannot go out. I cannot go to my field, for I am in chains."

The man threw himself back groaning on his bed. Eveli wanted to go. "Wait just a minute, just one minute," he asked. "Were you up on the mountain? How does the corn look? Is it already yellow? Oh, if I could see the ears!"

"Yes, I think it is already yellow in many places," said Eveli, "but I didn't notice it carefully, because I was only looking at the flowers; but tomorrow I will look at it specially, and then I will tell you."

"You are a good child; yes, come again and bring me the news," begged the sick man, "and will you bring me a cornflower, too, again, please?"

Eveli promised, and then as she went back through the ward

to leave them, the sick men all held out their hands to her and thanked her, and all begged her to come back again. Eveli was so filled with happiness and such great amazement, too, that she followed the sister as if in a dream. Never had she imagined that a man would thank her for a flower, and could take delight in it, and what gratitude and joy she had seen and heard from these beds of sickness! And that she could give this joy was an incomprehensible happiness for Eveli.

Then she came back again to Beni's room. He was sitting bolstered up with pillows, erect and comfortable in his bed as he had never been before, sitting in his wooden chair. Over the pretty coverlet was laid a flat, wooden board like a table, which was fastened to both sides of the bed. On this lay a lovely new slate and pencil beside it.

"See, see!" said Beni, beaming with joy; "Sister Marie brought me that, and she will allow you to come to me every day at two o'clock, and teach me and sing to me and tell me stories, as you did at home. I have told her all about it."

Eveli was so overcome at this new good fortune that she could not say a word, but with inexpressible satisfaction she looked first at the fine slate and then immediately at Beni, who was sitting so comfortably and fresh and clean in his bed. Eveli felt as if she must sing and shout aloud for joy. Beni said they might begin to study at once, for Eveli would have to show him what she had learned in school for five days. But then his nurse,

Sister Marie, who was always nearby in the room, came along and said today was Sunday, when no one studied. The children had so many days before them when they could continue their studies, it would be better today if Eveli would sing her songs, about which Beni had told her. The children were content with this, and Eveli began in the joy of her heart to sing her songs so blithely and gladly it was like a little jubilant lark soaring heavenwards and singing his songs above the cornfields and all the blue and red flowers blooming there. Beni could not have enough of it, for Eveli had never sung like this before. As soon as one song was ended he would say:

"Just one more, and then one more, and don't stop yet!" And Eveli went on singing with her clear voice until at last she said: "Now I don't know any more."

Without Eveli's seeing her, the sister had opened wide both doors to the adjoining wards. Then the pale woman lying nearest the door exclaimed: "This has been a beautiful Sunday! Bring her to us again!"

And other weak voices listening to Eveli said: "Sing once in here for us."

But then the sister came out and said it was time for Eveli to leave the hospital, but tomorrow and every day at this time she might come again, for she could see how all the sick people were looking forward to it with delight.

Eveli could not climb the mountain swiftly enough to tell her mother about all the wonderful occurrences which she had experienced in the hospital. Now she had a little time to listen; on Sunday evening there always came a time when her mother went around the house or stood in front of it in the vegetable garden by the gillyflowers without hurrying all her footsteps as on work days. Standing here in the vegetable garden, she listened silently to Eveli while she told with unusual vivacity about her experiences in the hospital and about Beni and his splendid bed and the firm pillows against which he could lean his weak back and be supported so finely. And as she pictured the other patients and their suffering faces, and then the delight they had shown at the sight of the flowers, there shot into Eveli's eyes such a wonderful gleam of love and sympathy that her mother looked at the child with astonishment. She had never seen her like this before.

"Tomorrow you must go and tell your grandmother all about it; it will make her happy," said her mother.

Eveli had well understood that her flowers had brought before the patients' eyes all the beautiful meadows and cornfields, and on that account they had been so unusually delighted. So on the following day, although she had picked just as large a bunch of the cornflowers as the day before, she gathered a quantity of the spicy-smelling thyme plants and placed them in her apron, for she could no longer clasp the bouquet together with one single long stalk with a full ear of corn on it. Eveli knew very well that one ought not to pull off the ears of corn, but she thought she might carry one single one to a sick man. The sweet-smelling thyme she thought would bring the shut-in invalids' eyes all the green hedges and sunny mountain slopes where it grew.

So Eveli came quite laden down into the hospital. The sister wanted to take her directly to Beni, but to her surprise she requested to go to the men's ward first. Here she went through the entire long ward to the last bed; there by the shaggy-looking bearded man she stood still.

"Here is an ear from the big cornfields in Mittelberg," said Eveli. "Here you can see how beautiful and yellow they are, and in the sunshine they are quite golden."

The man seized the stalk with a trembling hand and looked at the ear all around. The grains were firm and perfect; they only needed a little time before they would be fully ripe.

"Oh, how beautiful it is, a whole field of such ears. To see that!" said the sick man, groaning. "Did you say from the big cornfield in Mittelberg? Is it the one where the big oak stands in the middle, or on the other side where the lightning tore up the pear tree?"

"From the field where the big oak stands, I took the ear," said Eveli.

"It is from mine. So that is the way it looks, and I must lie here and cannot go out. Oh, my beautiful corn! My beautiful corn!"

Tears now stood in the eyes of the man who looked so wild. This went so to Eveli's heart that hers, too, filled with tears in a moment.

"Perhaps you will soon be well and can go out again," she said, trying to console him.

"You wish me well, that I see," said the man, wiping his eyes. "Come, sit down a little on the chair by my bed. Your flowers smell so good today. It seems like being up on the mountain. Have you thyme in your apron?"

Eveli said she had, and she opened her closely packed little apron. The strong odor floated through the room. Eveli heard how here and there a loud "Ah!" sounded, as if it were great refreshment to one and another.

In the next bed lay a young man, almost as young as Hans, but as thin and white as if he had never been in the sunshine. He quickly sat up in his bed and drew in long breaths of the fragrance.

"It smells like that at home in the garden," he said. "Ah, how long it is since I have seen it!

"It brings it all before my eyes, the wall where the thyme climbs up and the rushing brook behind under the alders."

The sick man turned away and buried his face in his pillow. Eveli rose and quickly laid a little bunch of thyme on his bed, then was going away, but the old man cried out:

"No, no! Not yet. Come, sit down again. I want to say something more to you."

Eveli obeyed.

"They say you sang beautiful songs in the other ward yesterday; sing one for us, too; we should like to hear it."

"Yes, we should like to hear it, too," said another patient; and Eveli began to sing the song about "Recovery." She thought perhaps that would please the old man the best.

"But tomorrow again, please, another song then, will you?" he asked; "and then another ear of corn, but not for a couple of days and not too much. And whose little girl are you that you come past Mittelberg?"

"The nettle-farmer in the forest," answered Eveli.

The sick man collapsed as if he had received a blow.

"That is not true!" he cried, his voice trembling with anger. "You don't belong to him! Perhaps you are staying with him, but you must belong to other people."

"Only to Mother," said Eveli, frightened.

The sick man looked at Eveli piercingly. "You do not look

one bit like him," he then said in a calmer voice. "Perhaps you are really like your mother. You must not be afraid of me; I will not hurt you. Come again, will you?"

Eveli promised that she would, quickly laid her flowers on all the beds, and went now to Beni.

It had grown somewhat late. Beni had been looking toward the door for a long time to see if Eveli was coming in. But when she told him what had detained her, he was quite satisfied and said he would willingly wait every day until she could leave the patients, for Beni knew about suffering and would gladly give pleasure to everyone who had to suffer. He was happy, too, and had so much to tell Eveli. She must know how often Sister Marie came to his bed and showed him how to make new strokes, and even whole letters, and had promised him an A-B-C book. Then it might really be that he could get ahead a little faster even than Eveli herself, he had so much time to study. He looked expectantly at his teacher.

At this news Eveli showed such great delight, and from her heart, that Beni dared express his real joy over it, for he had silently worried lest Eveli would be a little troubled if he went ahead of her. But Eveli felt nothing but the greatest delight when Beni read like a pupil in the sixth class.

When Eveli today left the hospital, she ran to her cousins' house. Her mother had told her the day before that she must go to her grandmother, and she herself wanted to go, for she must tell her everything. If only she should find her alone!

Sure enough, she was sitting quite alone in the living room at her spinning wheel.

"Grandmother," she exclaimed as she came through the door, "it has already happened, it is already there!"

"What? What?" asked her grandmother in astonishment.

"The blessing, you know—the blessing, which lies under the burden, that the dear Lord sent us," stated Eveli eagerly. "You know you said it was always lying under hard things to bear, although we might not see it right away, but at last it would appear, and with us it has appeared so soon!"

And Eveli began to tell the grandmother all about the blessing which had come to her herself, and first of all to Beni through the occurrence which had made them both so sad that they thought they never could be happy again. The grandmother was so delighted she could no longer spin, but could only listen and say again and again:

"Have you thanked the dear Lord? Don't forget to thank Him, Eveli!"

And when she had heard everything and had rejoiced with Eveli about it all, she said:

"You see, Eveli, when something hard comes to you again, and it will come many times, then think that the dear Lord has surely laid a blessing in it, but it will not always appear so soon as has happened this time nor always in such a way, for often it is a blessing which you cannot see at all; it may come entirely hidden from you, so that you never know when it is already there. You must never forget this, Eveli; then you can always be a little comforted, if trouble comes to you, and can think even if it is hard, I surely know that the dear Lord has in mind something good for me."

Eveli thought immediately that she would never, never forget this as long as she lived.

But the grandmother said it would not be as easy as she thought now, since she saw the blessing so plainly before her eyes. It was the same with other people, too. Whenever new trouble arises they see only that, and because of their sorrow no longer think how the dear Lord has meant it for us and always means it.

Chapter 5: The Nettle-Farmer's Surprise

Every day in the beautiful vacation time, Eveli came down to the hospital with a new bunch of flowers, and every day the patients looked forward to her appearance, so that one could see she brought everyone something that did them good. Above all, the old man in the corner awaited the child's coming with the greatest impatience and longing. As the time drew near he would call the nursing sister to him again and again and ask: "Has the child come yet?" And if Eveli was there, she had to sit down by him at once, and it would be a good while before she could come away. When he would beg her not to leave him, as he had nobody else in all the world to come to him and trouble about him, then Eveli would always sit with him longer and do everything he wished, and he said she helped him to forget his pain. Not only did Eveli have to sing him a few songs every day, but he had now found out that she knew how to tell pleasant stories. Eveli could never tell him enough stories, which she had heard from her teacher, and also about all the old events her grandmother had told her.

When the last week of vacation came to an end, he inquired of Eveli what would happen now, whether in spite of school she would be able to come to the hospital every day. She thought she would always come on the two afternoons when there was no school and also on Sunday; on the other days she could only come for a short visit, because it would usually be too late for her to go up the mountain alone.

Then she had to promise the sick man to come to his bed every time when she was there for a short while, and on free days always to stay longer with him. Eveli was heartily glad to promise everything; she knew no joy as great as this, to be desired by somebody and to be able to do him good.

On the last day of vacation the sick man had asked Eveli for all the songs he liked to hear her sing, and Eveli had had to stay with him still longer and tell him how it looked in the fields and meadows and on the trees on the whole mountain, and especially about the fields on the middle farm. When at last Eveli had to go, the sick man with difficulty drew a paper from under his pillow and said:

"There, don't lose it. Take it to your father."

Eveli placed it in her pocket and then ran to Beni in order to make a farewell visit to him. But it was no sad farewell; the children had no separation before them. Friendly Sister Marie had given Eveli permission to come to the hospital as often as she had time. There would be three entire afternoons in the week and many hours on other days, as Eveli hoped. Besides, Beni knew that he would no longer be as alone as formerly during school hours, Sister Marie was so kind to him. He did not dare to say how many letters of the alphabet, through her help, he could now make more than Eveli; he concealed his wealth like the most precious treasure. He surely hoped that

Eveli would gradually acquire the same treasure now that school was beginning again.

Eveli hurried home. But she had had so little interaction in her life with her father that she was afraid to give him the paper herself. She quickly sought her mother, told her what the man had given her, and asked her to hand it to her father. Her mother unfolded the paper and read what was written in it. Then she folded it up again.

"No, Eveli, you must give that to your father yourself," she said. "He is just coming in."

Then she went into the kitchen. Eveli stood anxiously with the paper in her hand when her father came in. Then she held out the note to him and said:

"The sick man told me to give you this."

"What sick man? What is this nonsense?" growled her father.

"I don't know," answered Eveli, still offering him the crumpled paper.

Then her father took it. He unfolded it. It was written over inside. The writing was large enough so he could easily read what it said. He read:

To the Nettle-Farmer:

You can have the piece of land today, if you like. You can thank your child, not me. She has done me good. I am surprised that you have such a child.

You can have the land at the first price that I valued it at. I will not make any profit from you, on account of the child.

Rall, the Middle-Farmer

The father looked over the letter at his child, as if he had never seen her before. He had really noticed her very little. One could see that he did not know where he was. He read the letter over again from beginning to end. At this moment the brothers also came in to supper. As they had been quarreling, they were both full of anger, and Heini, who now threw open the door and came in noisily first, actually almost fell over Eveli, for she was in a very unusual place by the door, as she was still standing in front of her father. She thought she ought to wait for an answer.

"Can't you ever keep out of the way!" screamed Heini "You good-for-nothing—"

Then their father struck such a frightful blow on the table with his fist that everything shook and the big boys cowered.

"If I ever one single time hear such a word from either of you two, I will show you who is master, so that you will think about it," he thundered. "Now you know it!"

The boys looked at each other in amazement. Neither of them could understand how their father's anger could have turned to the other side.

On the following evening, when the nettle-farmer had had time to realize his good fortune and also time to talk, for it was Sunday, he told his wife and his sons about the offer the middle-farmer had made him, but he did not bring out the letter. He intended to take the matter in hand without any delay, for a man who did business in such an inexplicable way might suddenly change his mind overnight. Something else the nettle-farmer had also in mind. The child, who had worked this change in the middle-farmer's decision, which he could hardly understand, deserved a reward; she must have it. When the nettle-farmer considered what he had offered for the land and what he would get it for now, he could afford to give a good reward without noticeably affecting the profit he would make. He thought the matter over for a day.

When Monday evening came, and he was entering the living room, he called to the child that he had something to talk with her about. Eveli came timidly out of the kitchen, where she was happily telling her mother about the new school day and her noonday visit to her grandmother. Cousin Hans had kept his word well; as soon as one of his brothers or sisters began to tease Eveli a little, he fell upon them in such a way that all the others had to stop laughing and give up teasing. So from now on she could go to her cousins' house without any fear, for Hans would always protect her.

"I have something to say to you," said her father, when Eveli stood in front of him; "you did a good thing, although I don't know how, but you deserve a reward. Tell me what you would like most. You can have it."

Eveli kept silent.

"Tell me what you would like. You needn't be afraid," said her father encouragingly. "I don't know what thing it would be. You have probably seen something down at your aunt's that would please you."

Eveli was still silent.

"Well, what is it? Can't you make up your mind?" asked her father. "Or don't you wish for anything?"

"I do wish for something," said Eveli timidly.

"Well, speak it out. I have promised you that you shall have it. Tell what it is," commanded her father.

"I should like to stay always in the hospital, like Sister Marie, and do everything for the patients to make them well," was the soft answer.

If Eveli had suddenly spoken Latin, her father would not have regarded her with such amazement as he did now. He did not know either about the hospital, or of Eveli's visits there, nor really anything about her life.

"I don't know what you are saying," finally he replied slowly, "about the hospital and what goes on there, only the pastor knows. Now wish for something that can be done."

"Ask the pastor," said Eveli.

Her father looked as if he had the same thought as the middle-farmer, as if he did not understand how this could be his child that would not open her hand to take the best thing when the very best was offered to her. But this firm persistency in the matter struck him as a family trait.

"She has become my best boy," he said to himself.

"All right, then, a promise is a promise," he said aloud and let Eveli go.

On Sunday he dressed in his church clothes early, for he was going to church, he told his wife, who was very much surprised, for her husband usually went there only on high festivals. But the nettle-farmer would not go to call on the pastor without going to church.

As soon as he came home he told his wife that after the service he had been to the pastor's, who had told him things he could hardly believe. He knew Eveli very well, and the pastor's wife knew especially about her. She went often to the hospital, had frequently seen the child there, and had noticed with surprise how much good she did to the patients. He had then told the pastor Eveli's wish, whereupon he had answered that they should tell the child that when she came to receive his instruction he would talk with her about the matter, and when she was confirmed she would learn that he had not forgotten her wish.

Until then the child should be allowed to go to the hospital as before; it was a comfort and delight to everybody. The pastor had talked about the child as of something unusual, to be taken great care of. No one had thought of such a thing, but yet they must see that the child was treated right at home, and they must not allow the boys to be unkind to her.

"We have been calling her by an outrageous name. We shouldn't have done so," concluded the farmer a little regretfully.

"Eveli has a good name, that is sure," said his wife, "and I will take good care of the child. I am delighted that our pastor has taken her under his protection and shown you that she is worth the care."

Eveli's mother told her what the pastor had said, and that her wish would be fulfilled as soon as it was time.

Autumn had now come. Eveli had only one hour to spend in the hospital, for she could not go home from school after dark. So often she did not know how to find time for Beni and the teaching which she had begun. The middle-farmer had made her promise to come to him every day, so she always went to him first and then could hardly get away from him. When she told the grandmother how emaciated the man looked, and how glad he was to hear her songs, she always tried to recall new stories about people she had known, who after penitence and sorrow for all the earthly wrongs they had done and suffered, had craved God's pardon, and had finally gone happily and peacefully to another life. Then Eveli would tell it all to the middle-farmer, who always liked to listen to the grandmother's stories.

When Eveli came in to Beni one evening and supposed that this time he would surely be cross because she came so late, Beni looked up at her with beaming eyes and exclaimed at once:

"Come, Eveli; today I have something to tell you; you can't think what it is! If only it doesn't make you feel badly."

"Anything that makes you so happy surely wouldn't make me feel badly," asserted Eveli.

"Only think, think, Eveli; I can really read. I can read a story and understand it all," and Beni drew his little book from under his pillow and showed Eveli a story which he had read through.

"Perhaps you will be able to do the same soon," he added consolingly. "You don't know at all how it is when you can read all alone, what is in the whole book, and then in all—all the books people have."

Then Eveli broke forth in such rejoicing over this news that Beni could see she needed no consolation because she had not gone so far. Eveli rejoiced that Beni now had such a resource when she could not come so often and never more would find the time long and be sad when he had to be alone. Beni, however, had not imparted all his good fortune. Today Sister Marie had told him that he would not have to go home all winter long, which he had feared above all. The prospect of the long tedious days in the dark living room or the cold bedroom had often filled him with dread.

"Oh, just think, Eveli," he exclaimed in beaming delight, "to stay here the whole winter, where it is bright and warm, and sit in this lovely bed, and never more shiver in the dark, and fall off from the chair, when it hurt me so! And I can always read stories, for Sister Marie will bring me another book when I have finished this one; she has told me so. There are really not many people as well-off as I, don't you think so, Eveli?"

Eveli was so immensely delighted at this piece of glad news that she could only keep saying the same thing again and again and exclaiming for joy over it.

Now Beni would remain under kind Sister Marie's care, and in the place where she liked best to come, and she could always visit him every day. The children both thought such joy as they felt today was the greatest good fortune they could have.

On the day when the first snow fell, the middle-farmer closed his eyes. His last word had been a word of blessing which he called after Eveli. A few hours before she had sat a long while by his bed. He had asked: "Sing to me 'Short is the night,'" and while Eveli did so, he seized her hand and held it closer and closer, as if the little hand was an anchor for him in the dark billows surging around him.

The hints which the doctor gave Sister Marie about Beni's condition made it easy for her to obtain what she herself wished, that Beni should never have to leave the hospital. It was the fulfillment of his only wish, and it made him one of the happiest people for the short time which he had to spend in this life. In his comfortable bed with the little table over it, on which his book lay constantly, he sat with a contented smile, sometimes talking with friendly Sister Marie, then buried for a long time in his book, until the moment when Eveli appeared, and then the liveliest conversation on both sides crowded out everything else.

Every day in the new summer Eveli appeared again with her big bunch of flowers, to the delight and refreshment of everybody. But the pastor does not forget Eveli's wish, which will be realized as soon as the right time comes for it.

The End

The Children's Carol

By Johanna Spyri

Translated by Helen B. Dole

© 2019 Jenny Phillips
Originally published in 1922
This unabrideged version has been updated with
mordern spelling and punctuation.

Table of Contents

Chapter First: Basti and Fränzeli Learn a Song........63

Chapter Second: Unexpected New Year's Singers......72

Chapter Third: One Surprise After Another............86

Chapter First: Basti and Fränzeli Learn a Song

In Bürgeln, the little village above Altorf, the green meadows with their fragrant grass and gay flowers are wonderful to look at and to wander through in summertime. Shady nut trees stand roundabout, and the foaming Schächen brook rushes past them down through the meadows, making wild leaps whenever a stone lies in its way.

At the end of the little village, where there is an old tower overgrown with ivy, a footpath follows the brook farther along. Here stands an extremely large, ancient nuttree, and under its cool shade travelers enjoy lying down and looking from beneath the shady seat up to the high cliffs, which rise above into the blue sky. A few steps away from the old tree, a wooden foot-bridge crosses the roaring brook halfway up the mountain where the path climbs steeply. There stands a little hut with a small shed beside it, and higher up, another, and still another, and then, as if thrown down on the mountain, the smallest of all, with such a low door that no person could enter it without bowing his head. The goat shed behind it is also so small that only the leanest goat can go in and nothing else.

The little hut has only two rooms, a living room and a tiny bedroom next to it, and opposite the door of the living room is a space where the little fireplace stands. In summer, the house-door remains open all day and makes the little room light. Otherwise it is very dark.

The haymaker Joseph used to live in the little hut, but he has been dead for four years, and now his wife and two children still live there: quiet, industrious Afra with Basti, a strong, healthy boy, and the younger Fränzeli, a delicate little girl with bright curls.

Joseph and Afra had lived very quietly and happily and only left their home when they went to church together. Usually Afra stayed in the house attending to her tasks, but Joseph went away in the morning to his work and came back at night.

When a little boy was sent to them, they looked at the calendar and, as they saw that it was Saint Sebastian's day, they gave the child his name. Then when the little girl was born on Saint Francis' day, they named her Francisca, which after the custom of the country became Fränzeli.

Since she lost her husband, the children were Afra's best possession, her great comfort and her only joy on earth. She kept her children so clean and neat that nobody would have believed that they came from the meanest little hut and belonged to one of the poorest women in the whole region.

Every morning she washed them with all care and combed Fränzeli's light blond curly hair so that she would not look unkempt, and every Sunday morning, one of the two little shirts, which each child owned, was washed, and over these was put Fränzeli's best frock, and Basti's trousers, made from his father's. Usually both of them wore nothing else, for shoes and stockings never were on their feet all summer long. In winter, their mother had something warm in readiness for them, but really not much. It was not necessary, for the children then almost never went out of the house at all. For this and all the necessary work which had to be done, Afra had to be busy early and late, and could take little rest for herself. But nothing was too much for her. If she only had her children with her, and both looked up at her with their merry eyes, she at once forgot all the weariness from which she longed to be free, and she would not have exchanged her children for any luxury in the world.

Moreover, every one who saw the children was pleased with them. When they came down the mountain, hand in hand—for Basti always held Fränzeli firmly by the hand as if to protect her—the neighbors who saw them pass by often said to one another:

"I have often wondered how Afra manages with her children. Since mine came into the world they have never looked so attractive as these two."

"I was just going to say the same," the other usually replied; "I will ask my wife how it happens."

The women, however, were not pleased to hear this, and said there was nothing to be done about it; some children were like that and others are different, and Afra must not think that beautiful children were of the greatest importance. But Afra did not think so by any means. She only desired, since the dear Lord had given her such lovely children, not to disfigure them with dirt.

When one of the neighbors said to her:

"Afra, your children delight me. The boy is like a strawberry and Fränzeli, with her delicate little cheeks and golden curls, is like an altar-image," then she would reply:

"If the dear Lord will only keep them well and make them good! I pray for this every day." And this she really did.

Almost five years had now passed since she had lost her husband. Basti had been six years old some time before, and Fränzeli five, but she was so delicately and slenderly built that she looked nearly two years younger than sturdy Basti with his strong limbs.

It was a cold autumn, and winter set in early and promised to be very hard. Already in October there was much deep snow and it did not go away. In November Afra's little hut stood so deep in it that one could hardly step out of it. Basti and Fränzeli sat in their corner by the stove and never went outdoors anymore. Their mother had to go out now and then but only did so when she no longer had a crumb of bread in the house.

It was almost impossible to go down the mountain, the snow lay so deep, and no one made a path except sometimes one single man, who lived still higher up, and in whose footsteps she tried to walk. But if fresh snow had fallen, she had to make her way herself and break out a path. When she returned home from these trips, she was often so tired, she had to muster all her strength not to drop. And yet there was no longer so much to do that she could not take a little rest.

But it was not weariness which often made her silent and give out so many heavy sighs when she finally sat down in the evening to mend the children's clothes. Heavy cares oppressed her and grew every day. Often she did not know how she could get a bit of bread. She so seldom had any work, and if she had no knitting or spinning to do for a whole week, she could buy no bread, and the little milk from the thin goat was all the food she had for the three of them.

So Afra, often for hours at a time in the night, was puzzled to know what she could do to earn anything, if ever so little, for three long winter months still lay before her. Usually when she put the children to bed and sat down beside them with her mending, she sang a song to them which lulled them to sleep. Now she sat silently and no song would rise from her heavy heart.

She was sitting thus one evening, silent and full of trouble, and outside the wind howled and shook the little hut as if it would overturn it. Fränzeli had already fallen asleep when her mother sat down beside her, for she was not disturbed even when the wind howled and whistled so cruelly. But Basti's eyes were still wide open and looked at his mother while she mended. Suddenly he said:

"But, Mother, why don't you ever sing anymore?"

"Oh dear," she sighed, "I can't sing any longer."

"Don't you know the song anymore? Wait, I will show you how it goes," and Basti sat right up in his bed and began to sing:

Night descends from darkening skies

Fields and woods caressing.

Lord, to Thee our prayers arise,

Give us now Thy blessing.

With a steady, clear voice, Basti had sung the verse through quite correctly, for he had heard it so many evenings from his mother, and she was quite surprised. Suddenly a thought came into her head.

"The dear Lord has sent it to me," she said, and looked with delight at her boy. "Basti, you can help me to earn something, so that I can have bread again for you and Fränzeli. Would you like to do it?"

"Yes, yes, I would! This very minute?" asked Basti in the greatest haste, and immediately jumped out of bed.

"No, no, get into bed again. Don't you see how cold you are?" And his mother quickly put the little one back under the covers.

"But tomorrow I will teach you a song, and on New Year's Day, you can sing it to the people. It will not be much longer until then, and they will give you bread and perhaps nuts."

Basti became so excited at the prospect of this reward and this important assistance that he could not go to sleep and asked again and again:

"Mother, is it morning yet?" But at last sleep mastered him and he closed his eyes.

In the morning he woke with the same thoughts with which he had gone to sleep, but he had to have patience, for his mother said:

"We can't sing until evening, for I have too much to do today."

So Basti whiled away the time by telling Fränzeli what his mother was going to teach him, and that he would then be able to bring home bread and perhaps nuts too. Fränzeli listened quite intently and she, too, could hardly wait until the evening.

When it had grown dark and their mother had finished all her tasks, she lighted the little lamp, seated herself at the table, and drew Fränzeli on one side of her, and Basti on the other. Then she began to work on the warm stockings which had to be knitted for Basti to wear on the expedition, and said:

"Listen to me very attentively, Basti. I will sing the first verse a few times, then we will try to see if you know it." And the mother began to sing. It was not long before Basti was singing with her, and suddenly Fränzeli began to join in quite eagerly. When the mother heard her, she nodded to her kindly, and when the verse came to an end, she said:

"That is right, Fränzeli. Perhaps you will learn it too."

When she had sung the verse several times together with them, their mother said:

"Now will you try it, Basti? Fränzeli will help a little too, won't you Fränzeli?"

She nodded gladly, and Basti began his song with a steady voice. But how astonished their mother was when Fränzeli joined in with her silver, clear little voice, which she had never heard like this before. When Basti sometimes failed to follow the melody, the little girl sang on like a bird that sings his melody without any difficulty, and quite correctly. Her mother was highly delighted. She had never thought that little Fränzeli would be able to help, and it sounded so sweet when the two sang together that she wanted to listen to them all the time. She had accomplished so much more than she had expected.

Every evening now they sang with all diligence, and when the week was at an end, the children could sing the whole song with all four verses without hesitation. That delighted them so much that when they came to the end, they always wanted to sing it over again from the beginning, and could not have enough of it. Their mother was very happy about it, for now she could be sure that the children would not break down even if she was not with them.

December had come, and the end of the year was near. One evening shortly before, the mother sat down with the children to see if they were quite sure of their song and began the tune, but they were always ahead of their mother. They were so sure and so eager that their mother had to hurry her time a little throughout to keep with them. Without hesitation they sang all four verses of their New Year's song. These were the words:

The Old Year now has taken flight,
The New Year is beginning.
We pray it bring you all delight
In working and in winning.

Now come the icy winter days,
The ground is hard and frozen.
For the dear Lord directs your ways
As His wise Love has chosen.

The hungry birds may search the ground
For seeds the trees deny them,
And even children wander round
For crusts to satisfy them.

But may the New Year bring you all
Great joy and richest treasure,
And if the Lord your friend you call
He'll help you in full measure.

Chapter Second: Unexpected New Year's Singers

New Year's morning had come. The mother went to church very early, for she never missed that. Then she began to wrap the expectant children in all the warm things which they had. To be sure, they were not much, but she had knitted a pair of warm stockings for Fränzeli too, who would surely need them today. Finally she took an old shawl, which she herself usually wore, wrapped it round and round Fränzeli, took her in her arms, and said:

"There, now we can go."

Basti went ahead and worked his way bravely through the deep snow down to the path along by the Schächen brook. Here he could walk beside his mother and had so many questions to ask about where they were now and what was going to happen that the time passed very quickly and, before he knew it, the long way lay behind him.

They had now reached the first houses of Altorf. The mother noticed at once that a crowd of children were on their way to sing their New Year's songs. They were coming in and out of all the houses. Afra went without delay to the large hotel, standing not far from the church by the old tower. Here it was quite still. The mother placed Fränzeli on the ground, unwrapped her, and then sent the children into the big house, telling them to begin their song as soon as they entered. She herself withdrew a little way behind the tower so that she could see the children when they came out again.

Basti, holding Fränzeli firmly by the hand, went into the house and immediately began to sing his song in a clear voice, and Fränzeli joined him quite melodiously. Then the door of the hotel opened, the people called the children inside, praised them for their singing, and into the basket which the mother had hung on Basti's arm came from here and there many pieces of bread, and now and then a bit of money. The lady of the house laid in a big handful of nuts and said:

"On New Year's Day you must have something besides bread!"

Then Basti thanked her in quite a loud voice and Fränzeli very softly, and the children, full of joy at their gifts, ran out to their mother. Then they went on to another house, but there were other children singing there, and others coming after, so that often a whole crowd was standing together in the same house. If they all attempted to sing together, the woman or her husband would come out and say they would rather give each a piece of bread than have such a noise. Often there were some of them who did not receive any gift and had to go empty-handed away. More than once, when so many were standing in front of a door, the woman would call Fränzeli to her and say kindly:

"Come, little one, you are almost frozen; you must have

something, but then go home. You are a shivering like a little leaf."

After the children had sung in five or six houses, and were coming out of another, their mother saw that they could not go on any longer. It was bitter cold so that she herself was almost frozen, and delicate Fränzeli was trembling in every limb, so that she could no longer sing. Basti as well was completely blue and had such stiff hands that he could not grasp the basket, but had to hold it out on his arm when he was about to be given something.

Now the mother quickly wrapped Fränzeli around and took her in her arms.

"And you, Basti," she said, "run along fast, so as to get warm again."

Then they ran without stopping until they were at home in their little hut, and all three sat down around the little stove close together until their hands and feet were warm again. Then Basti brought out the basket, as they had to see what was in it.

After their great exertion, the children received each a fine piece of bread and their nuts besides, and so they celebrated together a happy New Year's evening. The mother, too, was happy and thankful. Although she had not received any lasting help, yet she had bread enough for many days, and here and there a penny had been thrown into the basket, and she could make good use of these.

Really hard days full of trouble followed, and the mother often had to struggle with want and cold. But finally, the long winter came to an end, the warm sun appeared again, and the children could once more sit in front of the little hut and no longer had to shiver with cold. The goat was again let out, could eat the sweet, young grass, and gave a little more milk.

The mother was relieved of a great burden, as she no longer had to hunt everywhere for wood to warm the thin little house sufficiently, for now the sun shone warm in the windows and lovely mild air streamed in. But the mother had over-exerted herself so greatly all through the winter, and had taken so little food that she had come to the end of her strength, and even the warm spring sunshine could not bring it back again.

Still, she did not lessen her work and ceaseless activity from early until late, and if oftentimes she thought she would have to succumb from weariness and weakness, a great, inward anguish always urged her on anew, for she foresaw very well that if she could no longer support herself and her children, they would be taken from her by the overseers of the poor and would be provided for somewhere else, so that she could earn her bread at service. The thought was so terrible to her that she preferred to spend her last bit of strength.

Now the long, hot summer days had come. From the cloudless sky the sun sent fiery heat down on the steep mountainsides, on which the late hay lay everywhere, drying or already gathered into stacks. Afra, with her children, had climbed where, high up among the rocks, she owned a little bit of land, from which every year she obtained the winter fodder for her goat.

She had bound together the hay that she had made the day before, in order to carry home the warm, dry load on her head. Fränzeli clung fast to her mother's skirt, as she always did when she had no free hand, but Basti had to carry a little load of hay too.

When they reached home, the mother immediately brought out the milk, for they had eaten nothing since their scanty breakfast except a piece of bread, which they had taken with them, and now it was five o'clock in the evening. When the mother took the rest of the bread with the milk out of the cupboard, she saw for the first time how very little there was. Until she finished knitting the stockings ordered, she would have no money to buy bread, and yesterday and today she had not been able to knit on account of the work with the hay. The mother gave half of the small piece of bread to Fränzeli, the other to Basti and said:

"I know quite well that you are very hungry, but you see that I can't give you any more, for there is no more there. But this evening I will knit fast, then tomorrow I can give you a bigger piece."

Basti took his little piece gladly, but he did not take a bite of it, for he saw that his mother, after pouring milk into the bowls, which she gave to the children, sat down and laid her head in her hands. Basti watched her intently.

"Where is your bread, Mother?" he asked finally.

"I haven't any, Basti, but I am not hungry anymore. I don't need any," replied the mother. Then Fränzeli hurried to her and quickly put a little crumb which she had left into her mother's mouth, and Basti held out his piece to her and said pitifully:

"If you haven't any, you must be hungry, so we will share with you."

But his mother gave it back to him. "No, no, Basti, eat it gladly. You see I can't eat anything. I don't feel quite well. If I can go to the doctor tomorrow down in Altorf, he will give me something, for I can't go on like this."

The last words she spoke in a low voice to herself, and suddenly sank back with closed eyes. She had fainted from weakness and exhaustion.

Basti looked at his mother for a while, then he said softly to Fränzeli:

"Come. I know what I am going to do, but you must be very quiet, so as not to wake Mother. You see she wants to sleep a little while."

Whereupon he seized Fränzeli's hand firmly and led her to the door. She couldn't help being anything but quiet, for she had neither stockings nor shoes on her little feet, nor had Basti either. So they came very softly out through the open door and went together down the mountain. When they had left the steep mountain footpath behind them, and continued their way along by the roaring water, Basti pushed Fränzeli away from the brook to the other side of the path, and quite a good piece into the meadow, and said authoritatively:

"You see, Fränzeli, you must never, never, go on the other side, or you might fall into the brook. Mother said so, and little children like you would be drowned right away."

Fränzeli understood and willingly allowed herself to be led through the meadow. Then Basti went on to say:

"See, Fränzeli, now we are going into the houses in Altorf to sing our song again. Then we shall be given bread and perhaps nuts too. Then we will take everything to Mother, you know, because she couldn't get anything more to eat today. But can you still sing the song?"

Fränzeli was delighted at this prospect and went on with new eagerness through the meadow and then on the stony street, in spite of her bare little feet. She said she could still sing the song, and Basti began to try it once more. So the children sang their New Year's song loudly. They knew it still very well, sang it from the beginning through, and in this way came to Altorf before they knew it, although Fränzeli's tender feet had become quite red from the exertion. When they had reached the first houses of the place, they stopped singing and Basti said:

"I know very well which house to begin with, but not here."

He led Fränzeli, who was now rather tired, to the big hotel, "The Golden Eagle," where their mother had sent them in first on New Year's Day. But now it looked quite different from then. The evening sun threw golden beams on the open space in front of the door, and quite a noise came from there. A whole crowd of strangers had arrived, noisy young men in handsome, bright-colored caps, who, as soon as they came, had taken the large table from the dining room outside to the open square and were now sitting around it, eating and drinking in great merriment, for they had had a long walk today and were enjoying themselves. When Basti saw so many people at the table, and Fränzeli stood still from fright, he thought it better to sing to the men at a safe distance, so he began with all his might, that they might hear it even in the midst of the noise they were making.

"Be still," suddenly thundered the huge voice of a big, powerful man, who was sitting at the head of the table. "Be still, I say. I hear singing; we are going to have music at our supper table."

The men all looked around, and when they saw the children, who had placed themselves a little behind the old tower, they all beckoned to them, and a crowd of voices called together:

"Come here!" "Come nearer!" "Come right here!"

The children had stopped singing, and Basti came nearer very willingly, but he had to urge Fränzeli a little, for she was very much frightened.

Then the big blond man with the thick beard held out his long arm, drew Basti nearer to the table, and they all cried:

"Now let them sing, Barbarossa."

"There, now sing your song," he commanded, "only don't be afraid."

Basti began in a loud voice, and Fränzeli's small one was added like a soft, silver bell, and without hesitating they sang:

The Old Year now has taken flight

The New Year is beginning,

We pray it bring you all delight

In working and in winning.

"Mercy! We are on the other side of the globe. They are celebrating New Year's here!" exclaimed Barbarossa loudly, and such a shouting and laughing followed that they made a terrible noise.

"Listen and don't make such noise," cried the tall man with black, curly hair sitting next to Barbarossa. "Look at the little madonna; she is trembling from fright."

Then they were really quiet and all looked at Fränzeli, who was clinging anxiously to Basti.

"Maximilian, take the little girl," commanded Barbarossa, "and then let them sing again!"

Maximilian took Fränzeli kindly by the hand and said: "Come to me, little girl, then no one can hurt you."

Fränzeli held his firm hand trustfully, and as soon as it was quiet, Basti's voice continued singing:

Now come the icy winter days,

The ground is hard and frozen.

For the dear Lord directs your ways

As His wise Love has chosen.

"He really has protected me from cold today," exclaimed Barbarossa, who was all aglow—eyes, cheeks, and beard.

Noise and loud laughter broke forth again, but many of them cried out: "Again!" "Again!" "Once more!" The children sang:

The hungry birds may search the ground

For seeds the trees deny them.

And even children wander round

For crusts to satisfy them.

"That they must have; they must have that," they all cried from all sides, and a crowd of plates piled with good things was pushed towards the children. But Basti did not allow himself to be enticed away; with a steady voice he went on singing, and Fränzeli helped him to the end:

But may the New Year bring you all

Great joy and richest treasure,

And if the Lord your friend you call

He'll help you in full measure.

Then a tremendous shouting broke forth, and all cried together:

"That is a beautiful wish! That will bring us good luck on our journey!"

But Barbarossa now drew Basti to him and placed before him a plate filled with fine things such as he had never seen in all his life before. On the edge lay a large piece of snow-white bread, and Barbarossa said encouragingly:

"There, my son, now go bravely to work and don't stop until you have finished everything."

And all the other plates heaped high were pressed towards him, and from all sides they cried: "Take this too!" "He shall have this one too!"

Basti stood and gazed at all the luxuries, his eyes shining with delight and growing bigger and bigger with expectation, but he did not move. Fränzeli's protector, whose hand she still held fast, had placed a plate just as abundantly filled before her and urged her to help herself. Fränzeli, who had grown very hungry during the long walk, immediately took a fine morsel on her fork and was going to put it in her mouth, but she quickly glanced at Basti, and when she saw that he was not eating a single mouthful, she hastily laid her piece back again on the plate.

"What is the matter with you? Why don't you begin to eat, my brave son of William Tell? What is your real name?" asked Barbarossa.

"My name is Basti," was the reply.

"Good, Basti, my son, what are you thinking about so deeply that makes you open your eyes so wide and takes away your appetite?"

"If I only had a bag!" he burst forth.

"A bag? And what for?"

"I would put everything into it and take it to Mother. She has no more bread today."

Then the men became quite sympathetic, and many of them cried out that they must get him a bag and he must do as he wished. Others asked where his mother lived, if she was quite near. When Basti answered that she lived in Bürgeln up on the mountain, they all exclaimed in surprise and Barbarossa said:

"If you have come down from there, you must really be hungry—is it not so, Basti?"

"Yes, and besides because we have had only a very little bread all day," he stated, "but tomorrow, perhaps, Mother can finish the stockings, and then we shall have more."

Then each of the men wanted to do something, one to get a bag, others a porter, but Barbarossa called out above all the others:

"Now first of all, I want to see that these two children have enough to eat, and then the rest will come later. Now listen, Basti! What is here on your plate is yours. Eat that and when you have finished, your mother shall have all the rest."

"Everything?" asked Basti, and looked with shining eyes at all the well-filled plates.

"Everything!" stated Barbarossa. "Can you begin now?" Then

Basti seized his fork and ate with such a satisfactory appetite that Barbarossa looked on with great delight, and Maximilian sympathized as he also urged Fränzeli at last to appease her great hunger. The proceeding was interrupted now and then by a short question and answer.

"Did your mother send you here to sing the song?" asked Barbarossa.

"No, she went to sleep, because she had no bread to eat and was tired. She wanted to go to the doctor, too, because he would give her some medicine," explained Basti, "and so I came with Fränzeli, so that Mother could have some bread when she woke, because we got bread the first time when we sang here."

Then the men understood how it had happened that the children had sung their New Year's song to them, and Barbarossa said:

"I propose that we all together accompany our singers up to Bürgeln. Besides, tomorrow we must look for the place where the wild waters of the Schächen brook swallowed up the brave Tell. Today let us make a moonlight party and bring our runaway friends back to their mother."

"And you, as the kind doctor, can give her a good prescription," added Maximilian.

Chapter Third: One Surprise After Another

Meanwhile, the mother had half awakened several times but did not have the strength to recover herself, and each time fell back again and lay for several hours in a sort of stupor. Finally, she awoke. The twilight had already come on. She could not see her children, but she was so tired that she remained sitting. "Basti!" she called after some time, as everything was so still around her. "Fränzeli, where are you?"

She received no answer. Then her anxiety gave her strength. She rose quickly, went to the house door, but there was nobody—she went to the goat and it was all alone—then around the hut, calling the names of the children again and again—all was still. Only from below roared the wild raging Schächen brook. A frightful anguish came over the mother, and she could hardly keep on her feet. She folded her hands and fervently besought the dear Lord to spare her from the worst. Then she ran along the footpath and was going down the mountain when she saw a whole procession of people coming up from below. All were talking loud and eagerly together, and it seemed exactly as if their raised walking sticks were pointing to her hut.

"Oh, merciful goodness!" she said in the greatest alarm. "Can it be a message for me?" She could not take another step farther, but stood as if paralyzed.

"Mother! Mother!" she suddenly heard called from below. "We are coming now, and you must see what we are bringing! And the men are all coming with us, and Fränzeli is coming in a carriage with a horse."

Now Basti rushed ahead of all the others and kept calling out and breathlessly telling everything that had happened, for he could not wait for his mother to learn all. And when he had finally reached the top and rushed to his mother, she pressed the boy to her and thanked God with all her heart, and the delight gave her new life.

But her astonishment and surprise grew with every moment, for behind Basti came a whole crowd of men, and they all greeted her in the most friendly way, like old acquaintances. Two of them were carrying on two walking sticks, which rested on their shoulders, a huge basket, and finally came a man holding Fränzeli by the hand, and the child, usually so shy, was so trustful with him that she did not once let go of his hand when she saw her mother, but pulled him along to her.

Good Afra did not know when she should begin to thank them, for from Basti's talk, she quickly grasped that the men had shown every sort of kindness to the children, and the well-filled basket showed it also. She turned at once to Barbarossa. Because he was the largest of them all, she took him for a sort of leader and thanked him so heartily that he was much moved.

Then it suddenly came to his mind that he ought to give her some medical advice and proposed to her to step inside the hut with him and to tell him what was the matter with her. She was very much delighted at this and inside explained to him that she really had no pain but could hardly stand and walk from weakness and lack of strength. He asked her then what she was eating and drinking and she told him everything. Then Barbarossa stepped out in front of the hut and called in a loud voice:

"Bring the medicine here!" He himself ran hurriedly to collect it, and to Afra, who was speechless with amazement, he said:

"You see, my good woman, we have brought the medicine with us. Take a good spoonful every day and then you will be better."

"Oh, my dear sir," Afra was a last able to bring out, "thank you so much. So much!"

"My worthy woman," replied Barbarossa, "you are most, most welcome! And now fare you well and your children too!"

Whereupon he reached out his hand to Afra, and she followed him out and took leave of all the men, but she could not finish thanking them. Fränzeli, too, now thanked her protector as well as she could and begged him to come again soon. Basti ran from one to another with his thanks and hurried to the outermost point of the cliff and screamed with all his might as long as he could see anything of the men:

"God bless you, Barbarossa! God bless you, Maximilian!" For he had learned their names well.

When the children were sitting with their mother inside the hut, they had so much to tell her, how everything had happened, how they had quickly gone away to get her a little bread by singing while she was asleep, and how then one thing after another had occurred, until they had been brought home with the horse and the carriage. Fränzeli could hardly find words to describe the grandeur she had felt in driving home in the wagon.

Now the big basket was unpacked, and out of each package rolled new and wonderful things to eat, and finally at the bottom came into sight three whole loaves of white bread, which the men had placed there especially. Then Basti was so overcome with delight that he made the highest leaps around the room and had to shout aloud again and again:

"God bless you, Maximilian! God bless you Barbarossa!"

But the mother said over and over:

"The dear Lord put this into the young men's hearts. We will pray for them every day, my children, and never forget them."

Meanwhile the students were making their way in great hilarity down towards Altorf. Only Maximilian was quite silent for a while, and then he suddenly broke out with the words:

"It really is not right! No, it is not right. We have only rescued the woman and children from dying of hunger, and gone no further. What will they do in the winter without warm clothes, without food, without everything? That must not be. We must take up a collection right away, today, and the hotel keeper will hand over the proceeds."

"Maximilian," replied Barbarossa, "your intention is good, but the proposal is impractical. You forget that we are travelling, that we are far from home and will need much more to get there. What will be left to collect? I will make another proposal. Let us form a society, the Bastiania—yearly dues: four marks. All our mothers and sisters shall be named honorary members, who will supply the necessary blouses and dresses for Basti and the little girl. As soon as we reach home, the honorary members will be called to assist in the work of love, and the first contribution from the Bastiania will be sent off."

This proposition found great approval. In the gayest spirits the students entered Altorf again, found their table still standing outside, seated themselves once more at it, and here in the bright moonlight, the Bastiania Society was founded and started.

How amazed Afra was when some weeks later the postman

brought up such a mighty big package to her that he had to push it through the door with all his strength. Then he threw it on the floor and said, knitting his brows:

"I am wondering, Afra, what acquaintances you have so far away in Germany. The postmaster, too, couldn't guess who you could know so far away."

"Perhaps you haven't come to the right place with the package," replied Afra.

To be sure, Afra's name and her residence were plainly marked on it. She loosened the firmly sewed corner and the whole fastening became gradually undone. The children looked with great excitement at the mysterious object. Suddenly it all fell apart and out rolled blouses and frocks and shawls, shoes and stockings, to their great astonishment, and in the midst fell out a heavy roll, in which were many, many silver pieces. The mother clapped her hands together and kept exclaiming:

"But where did they come from? Where did such a blessing come from?"

Then Fränzeli brought her a sheet of paper, which had fallen out of the things. On it stood the words:

And if the Lord your friend you call

He'll help you in full measure.

Then Basti immediately cried out: "That is in the song; it has come from the men!"

"Yes, it must be so." Now it was clear to the mother, too, that the rich gift could have come from no one else but their benefactor. What inexpressible gratitude now filled her heart, when she suddenly became entirely free from the great anxiety, lest she be separated from her children. Now she had such abundant supplies she could live without care the coming winter.

How astonished Afra was when the next year, a similar package came again, and every year following. For the Bastiania Society continued as a solid alliance, and the honorary members thought, with each frock and jacket their children outgrew, of the little New Year's singers, who had been pictured in such glowing colors to them by their sons and brothers on their return from their trip to Switzerland.

Afra had hung up in her room, as a continual remembrance, the sheet of paper, which the men had placed in their package, and on the which stood the words:

And if the Lord your friend you call

He'll help you in full measure.

More Books from The Good and the Beautiful Library!

Just David
by Eleanor H. Porter

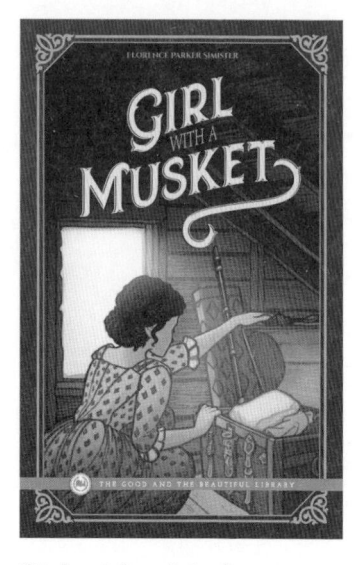

Girl with a Musket
by Florence Parker Simister

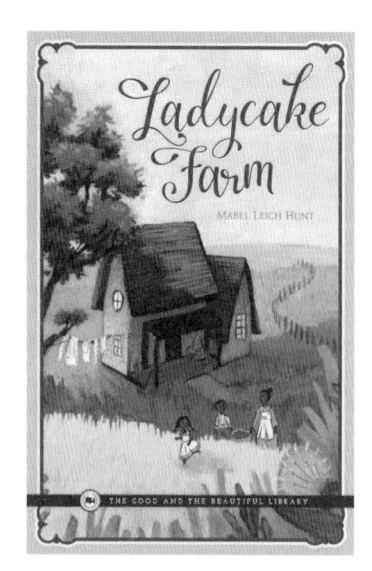

Ladycake Farm
by Mabel Leigh Hunt

Tiger on the Mountain
by Shirley L. Arora